201 English Activity Book

N	P	R	O	N	O	U	N	K	O
O	C	V	O	W	E	L	S	L	P
U	M	A	R	T	I	C	L	E	P
N	K	L	H	O	A	T	X	M	O
A	D	J	E	C	T	I	V	E	S
D	X	H	A	O	A	P	E	A	I
V	L	T	C	A	K	A	R	X	T
E	O	A	L	M	P	A	B	H	E
R	R	H	Y	M	E	S	E	P	L	S
B	M	H	X	T	T	C	O	K	A

Wonder House

1. Trace and follow the small letters of the English alphabet to help the monkey reach his home.

2. Help the snail reach the flowers by completing the alphabet trail.

3. Connect the dots of the letter trail to get a whale and color it inside the ocean.

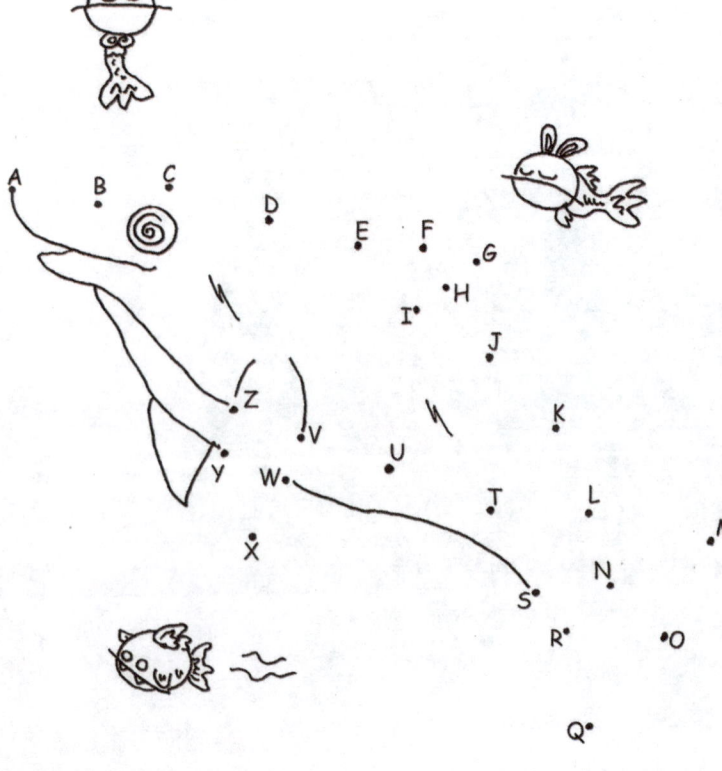

4. Write the missing beginning letter of each object.

.... omb

.... oor

.... og

.... us

.... ed

.... all

5. Follow the letters of the English alphabet to help the dog reach his bone.

6. Match the capital letters with the correct small letters and then color the objects.

7. Circle the first letter of these objects.

U V X

V Z W

W X V

U X Z

Y R S

Z V U

8. Place the given letters in alphabetical order.

③

9. Fill in the blank coaches with the correct capital letters and complete the alphabet train.

10. Match the capital letters with the correct small letters and then color the objects.

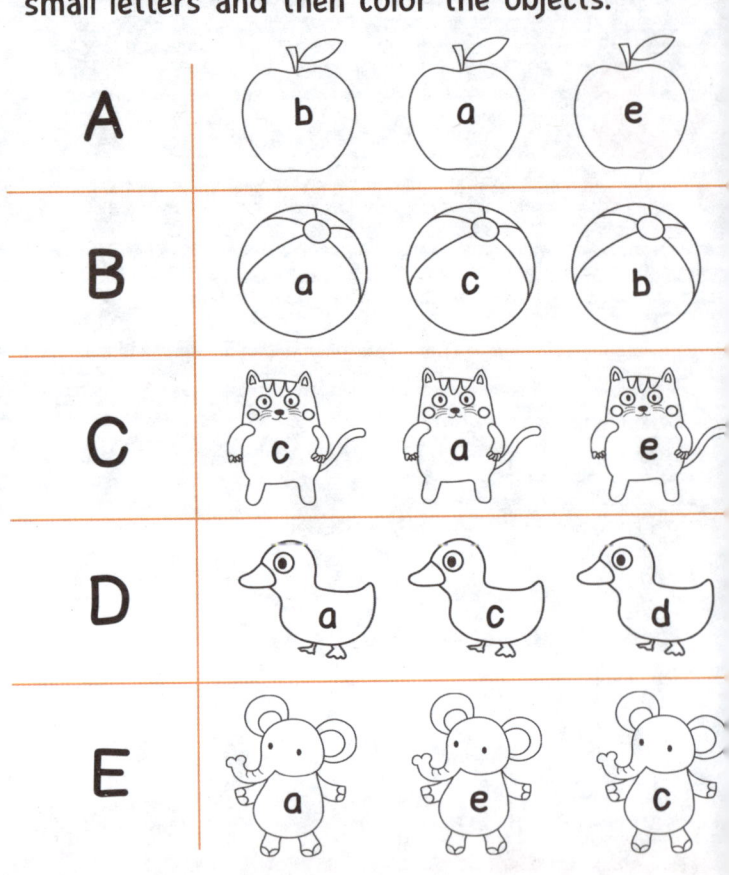

A	b	a	e
B	a	c	b
C	c	a	e
D	a	c	d
E	a	e	c

11. Trace the capital letters on the left. Circle their small letters on the right.

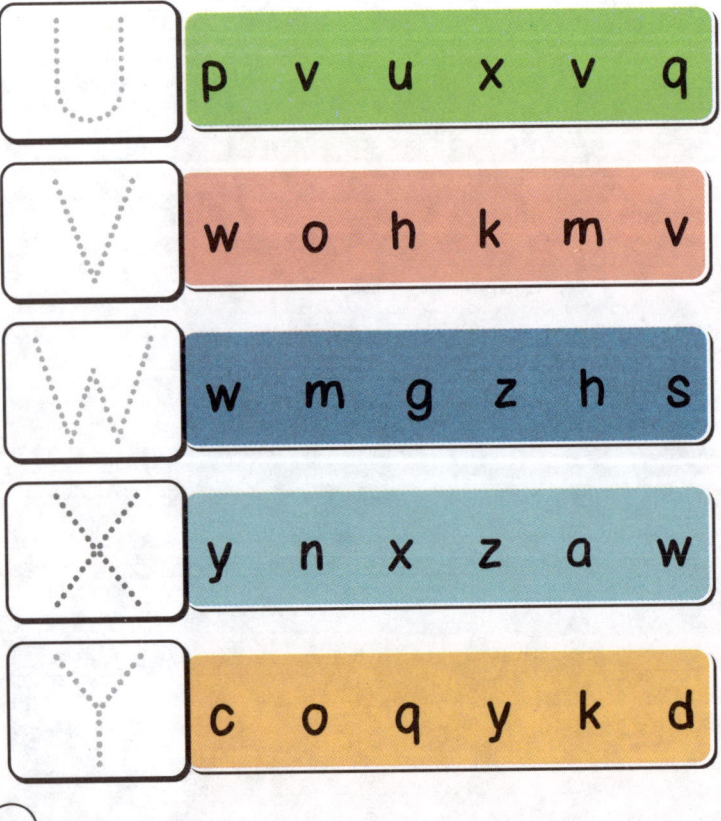

U	p v u x v q
V	w o h k m v
W	w m g z h s
X	y n x z a w
Y	c o q y k d

12. Fill in the blanks with the correct last letters

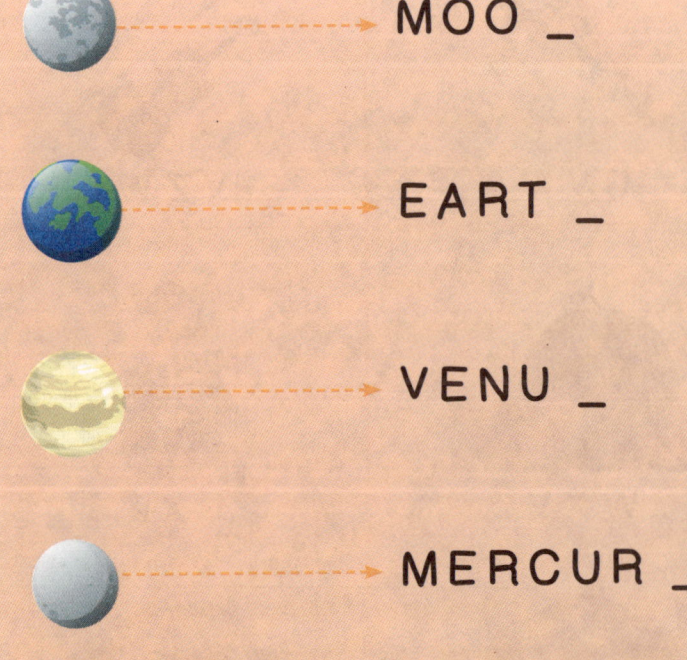

MOO _

EART _

VENU _

MERCUR _

MAR _

13. Identify the picture and circle the first letter.

K N O   M L N

M O P   L N F

14. Fill in the missing small letters in the cupcakes to get all the alphabet.

b   e

g

j   l   n

r

u

x

15. Fill in the blank spaces with the right letters to make words.

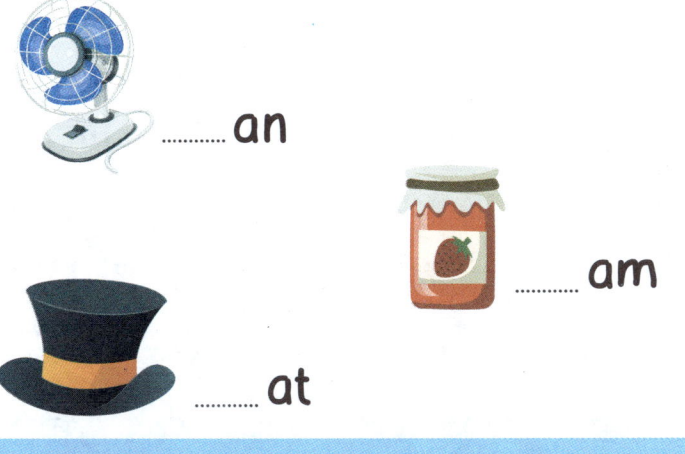

..........an

..........am

..........at

16. Match the letters with the animals.

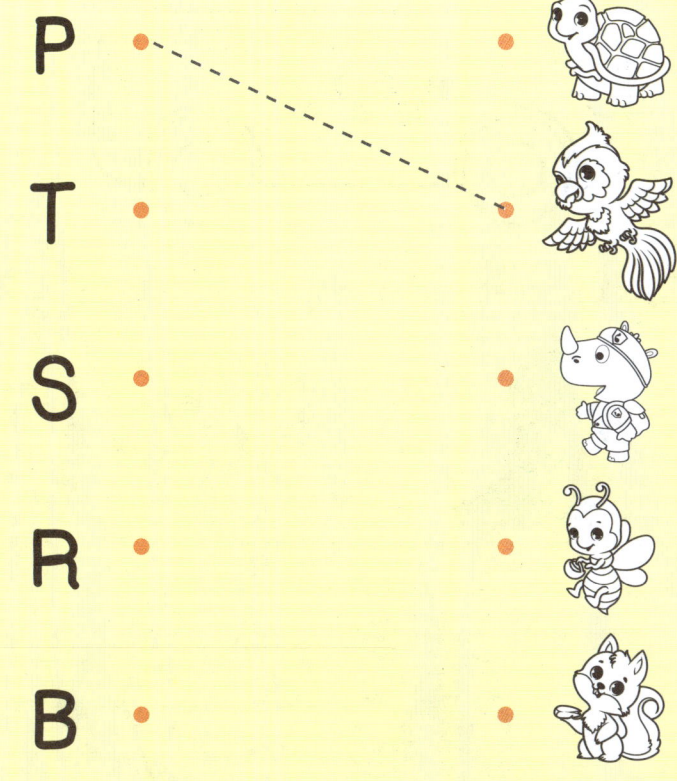

P
T
S
R
B

17. Fill in the boxes with the correct letters.

a

q u e

18. Fill in the blanks with the missing letters.

 _ gloo

 is _ and

 ho _ se

 mou _ e

 ice cre _ m

 _ oma _ o

 ju _ ce

 pump _ i _

19. Write the missing letter. Color the vehicle.

 TAX _

20. Circle the words ending with a-e-i-o-u. Write the words you found in the given space.

The alphabets a, e, i, o, u in the English language are known as Vowels.

Tomato   Rainbow   Idea   Sun   Frill

Kettle   Media   Cup   Volcano   Soup

Pen   Banana   Bottle   Emu   Lake

You   Theatre   Bonsai   Piano   Ski

Tea   Plateau   Dice   Litchi   Video   Plain

-a	-e	-i	-o	-u

21. Choose the correct vowel.

a e i o u   a e i o u

a e i o u   a e i o u

22. Write the numbers in words.

....

23. Name the fruits.

....

....

24. Make new words from the given ones.

TAR _____

SIGN _____

TEN _____

STAN _____

NAP _____

25. Fill the boxes with the missing vowels.

	N	G	E	L
C				
O				
R				
N				

	A	G	L	E
L				
F				

	N	D	E	R
N				
C				
L				
E				

	S	L	A	N	D
C					
E					

	C	E	A	N
T				
T				
E				
R				

	N	S	E	C	T
R					
O					
N					

26. Read aloud the words in the grid and circle the ones you spot in the picture.

hut	bed	jug
dip	dam	log
sun	mat	top
fan	man	fig
boy	tub	cat
girl	dog	bin
web	egg	cap

27. Circle the words that begin with a consonant sound.

> All the letters in the alphabet apart from the vowels a, e, i, o, and u are known as Consonants.

Toucan   Panda   Under   Carrot

Mango   Tiger   Otter

Orange   Igloo   Tomato   Eagle

Donkey   Ape   Ice Cream

Umbrella   Sky   Gorilla   Spoon

Love   Ink pot   Airplane

28. Look at the pictures and fill in the missing consonants to complete each word.

F _ O _ E _

C _ E _ R _

_ R E _ S

_ T A _

> Sound blends are a set of two or three consonants that when pronounced together, retain their sound. Blends are found either at the beginning or at the end of a word.

29. Write three words for each sound blend.

br

ng

st

30. Match the blends on the left to the letters on the right to complete each word.

st •   • ider

sn •   • um

sp •   • ipt

gr •   • ail

gl •   • ork

scr •   • oves

fr •   • own

dr •   • ass

br •   • uit

31. Fill in the blanks with the correct sound blends.

1. The _ _ og came out of the water.

2. _ _ ink one glass of milk everyday.

3. _ _ ush your teeth daily.

4. He was born with a silver _ _ oon in his mouth.

32. Can you write 5 words with a vowel in the middle? Say the words out loud as you write.

33. Sort the jumbled words with double letters zz, ll, ss, oo, ee, & ff. Write them in the given space.

dam, under, bee, buzz, igloo, tree, full, teeth, fluff, face, bell, toss, skull, cliff, hoop, food, puzzle, red, yak, brass, sharp, candy, touch, green, floss, staff, blizzard

zz _____

ll _____

ss _____

oo _____

ff _____

ee _____

34. Jake is adding the letter e to his words. Can you help him? Read the words aloud before and after adding e and observe how they change.

TAP _	KIT _	ROB _	HOP _	CAP _
↓	↓	↓	↓	↓
....	....	....	....	....
				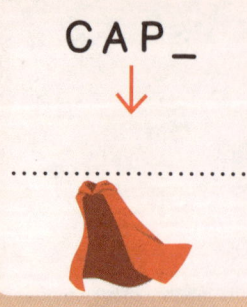

35. Choose the right spellings to spell the words correctly.

AY or AI	OI or OY
T _ _ L	B _ _ L
R _ _ N	_ _ L
D _ _	T _ _
S N _ _ L	E N J _ _
H _ _	C _ _ N
V _ _ N	N _ _ S E

36. Circle the words that are spelled correctly.

Rhythm/Rithm	Ginger/Gynger
Pyramid/Piramid	Bicycle/Bicicle
Single/Syngel	Angel/Eangle
Eagle/Eagel	Flying/Flyeeng
Saucer/Sauscer	Locket/Lauket
Zinger/Zingre	Please/Pleez

37. Help Danny choose i or y to complete the words.

W R _ T E R	R O _ A L	P R _ M E	T _ P E
A B _ S S	M _ L D	G _ M	D O L P H _ N
S _ N K	_ E L L O W	F _ N A L	H _ P E

38. Complete the words by adding a vowel.

J _ R

R _ T

_ C E

39. Can you think of some double letter words? Say each word aloud as you write.

40. Write two rhyming words for each in the jar.

 FAN

 HOLE

 PLACE

 COOK

41. Match the pictures with the words that rhyme. Say the words out loud.

   COAT

TOAD

   TREE

SOCK

   TOP

FEEL

   BLUE

PAIL

DIG

RACK

42. Write the word that rhymes with the word in red.

The **pot** is h _ t.

There is a **mouse** in the _ o u _ _.

The **frog** jumped over the _ o _ .

The **king** likes to s _ n _ .

My **coat** is in the b _ _ t.

Keep the **fish** in the _ i s _.

43. Identify each picture. Then, write the word and add 'e' to make a new word.

 .... + E ....

 .... + E ....

 .... + E ....

 .... + E ....

44. Write plurals of the following.

Shoe	Tree	Leaf	Man	Knife

....	....	....	....	....

45. Place these words correctly.

Cows Doll Cup Rabbits
Dog Chairs Cars
Cherry Cake Knives

SINGULAR

....

....

PLURAL

....

....

47. Can you think of some words that rhyme with 'rain and door'?

46. Fill in the missing letters using the picture clues.

STR _ _ _ _ _ RRY

U _ _ _ _ ELL _ _

N _ _ S _ _ _ _ ER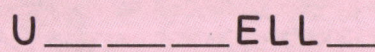

48. Match the rhyming words.

   •   •

   •   •

   •   •

   •   •

   •   •

49. Complete the sentence by writing plurals in the blanks.

1. One cherry. Four _____

2. One car. Six _____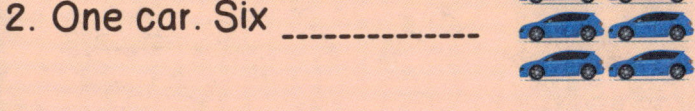

3. One puppy. Two _____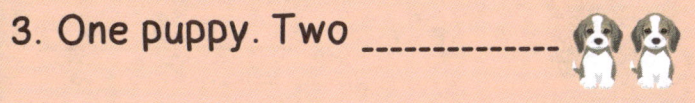

4. One cake. Five _____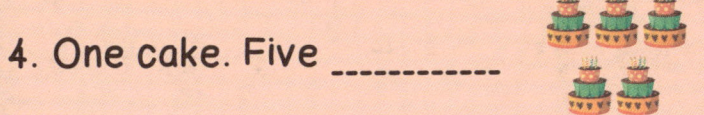

5. One person. Three _____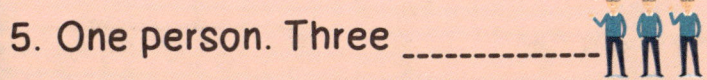

6. One plate. Four _____

50. Choose the correct option to describe the pictures.

Deer / Dear ....

Bare / Bear ....

Right / Write ....

51. Color the cup blue if it has a vowel under it.

52. Complete the rhyme using the words from the box.

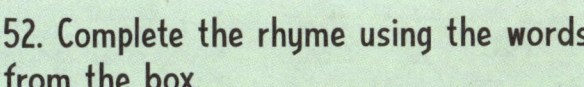
Rain Crawled Spider
Spout Again Dried

The itsy bitsy spider _____
up the water _____.

Down came the _____,
and washed the spider out.

Out came the sun, and _____
up all the rain.

And the itsy bitsy _____
went up the spout _____.

53. Count the syllables in each word and then draw a line to match with the right number.

> Syllable is a word or part of a word with a vowel sound formed by the opening and closing the mouth. The number of the vowel sounds heard in a word will determine the number of syllables the word will have.

Cobweb ●   ● 4

Animal ●   ● 1

Lunch ●   ● 2

Caterpillar ●   ● 3

54. Look at the pictures and unscramble the words.

 TBA _____

 NVA _____

 MPLA _____

 KSDE _____

 NMA _____

 ITKE _____

55. Let's find how many syllables are there in each word.

gar-den	horn	muf-fin	drag-on-fly	pear	bas-ket
 ☐	 ☐	 ☐	 ☐	 ☐	 ☐

> A compound word is formed when two words are combined to make a new word.

56. Observe carefully and write the compound words in the space provided.

sun + flower = ...

star + fish = ...

blue + berry = ...

air + plane = ...

water + melon = ...

57. Challenge yourself! Write all the compound words you can think of in 2 minutes.

58. Look at the pictures and write the new word for each pair.

....

....

....

....

59. Read aloud each word and write the syllables.

Children ....

Letter ....

Movie ....

Chicken ....

Underground ....

Banana ....

Watermelon ....

Monkey ....

Chimpanzee ....

60. Underline the compound words in the given sentences. Write the words in the given space.

1. Rocky found a pencil near a riverbank.

       =   +

....

2. Nina eats a strawberry a day.

       =   +

....

3. Tom went to Italy in an airplane.

       =   +

....

4. Pam made a pancake for breakfast.

       =   +

....

5. A butterfly has beautiful wings.

       =   +

....

6. Mary is playing in the backyard.

       =   +

....

61. Write 3 singular words that you can think of and then write their plurals in the baskets.

SINGULAR

PLURAL

62. Match the rhyming pairs.

Class •   • Cat

Night •   • Floor

Bat •   • Bake

Door •   • Grass

Face •   • Flight

Cake •   • Chase

63. Count and write the syllables in each word.

TUNA ....

SEAL ....

FISH ....

OCTOPUS ....

OYSTER ....

WHALE ....

DOLPHIN ....

SHRIMP ....

64. Complete the word sums to make new words.

RATTLE +
SNAKE =

....

ARM +
CHAIR =

....

BASE +
BALL =

....

RAIN +
COAT =

....

EAR +
RING =

....

SKATE +
BOARD =

....

BODY +
GUARD =

....

LAP +
TOP =

....

65. Read the sentence aloud. Can you count and write the vowels and consonants in this sentence?

ALY IS A CUTE GIRL.

VOWELS:

CONSONANTS:

66. Add s or es to the words to turn these into plurals.

Feather + _____ = _____

Boy + _____ = _____

Animal + _____ = _____

Bus + _____ = _____

Zoo + _____ = _____

Match + _____ = _____

House + _____ = _____

Quiz + _____ = _____

Brush + _____ = _____

Carrot + _____ = _____

67. Fill in the missing blends to complete each word and sentence.

1. Raja _ _ ives the car slowly.

2. Aliens travel in a _ _ aceship.

3. _ _ icks are used to make buildings.

4. Mike used _ _ ayons for coloring.

68. Look at the picture and fill in the missing letters. Then, put a '/' to separate each syllable in the word.

_ R A _ G _

69. Can you put these things in the right box?

cup, books, bag, scissor, shells, cake, bat, balloons, necklace

SINGULAR

PLURAL

70. Choose the correct word to complete the sentences.

| Orange | Fish | Books | Home |

1. A _____ can swim.

2. The _____ is sweet.

3. This is my _____.

4. I like to read _____.

71. Complete the sentences using "a" and "an".

1. We are going for _____ movie.

2. I ate _____ orange for breakfast.

3. Can I borrow _____ pencil?

4. It's _____ beautiful day!

5. Could you get me _____ ice cream?

72. Rewrite the jumbled sentences.

is my cat This.

_____

fun Reading a activity is.

_____

won quiz Jake the.

_____

pants blue The made are of cotton.

_____

73. Place the words next to the correct animal.

| Grass | Loyal | Bone |
| Neigh | Hoofs | Paws |

....

....

....

....

....

....

74. I have a trunk and two tusks. I am huge. Who am I?

_____

75. I have gills and scales. I swim in water. Who am I?

_____

76. How many animals can you name for each category?

SEA ANIMALS	WILD ANIMALS	FARM ANIMALS

77. Add the vowel 'a' and write the words below.

1. _____   4. _____

2. _____   5. _____

3. _____

78. Join the given words to make one word.

Butter + Cup	Egg + Shell	Basket + Ball	Flower + Bed	Rain + Bow

79. Write the synonyms of the given words.

Pretty Cheerful Unattractive Make Big

Ugly ....

Beautiful ....

Create ....

Huge ....

Happy ....

80. Fill in the blanks with 'a', 'an', or 'the'.

____ car is damaged.

I found ____ umbrella on the street.

Can I borrow ____ safety pin?

____ airplane is flying in the sky.

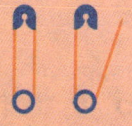

81. Read the clues to find the double letter words that are hidden in the word search. Write the double letter word in the space next to each clue.

```
C U F F S G N I G G I D
I I J A Y P D U C L I N
T U D H T U L I P E O O
E T V S H E L L E B W I
S L I V B I A R S N Q S
E U H E U E T A S S D M
V N C N O O N S K S Y U
D G L A S S E S S A N F
A H A Z K U M L S R A F
I Q Z P L A E A A G S I
D A Y C S J N B L P T N
J U W O O L T A M E Y C
```

1. You wear these when your eye sight is weak ....

2. Found on beaches and sea shores ....

3. Antonym of short ....

4. A plant grows up to become this ....

5. End part of a sleeve that has buttons over it ....

6. 12 'o clock in a day ....

7. All cows eat this ....

8. A kind of music genre originated in the US ....

9. Sweaters are knitted of this material ....

10. A Cupcake is also called ....

82. Read the rhyme and fill in the missing letters. Take help from the word bank.

DO, ASLEEP, MAT, PLAY

Nim, the cat was round and fat
He slept all day on a blue _ a _.

Ardy, the rat said, 'Hey, let's pl _ _!'
But Nim just slept the day away

Ardy was sad that Nim was a _ l _ _ p
He got so mad, he started to weep.

Then Ardy said, 'Wait, I don't have to be blue
I will play by myself. That's what I'll d _!'

83. Draw a line between the two words to form a new word.

Note •   • Boat

Book •   • Paper

Sub •   • Berry

Head •   • Light

House •   • Book

Sand •   • Shelf

Straw •   • Way

Cow •   • Mill

Sun •   • Glasses

Wind •   • Boy

84. Write the words from activity 83 in the notebooks.

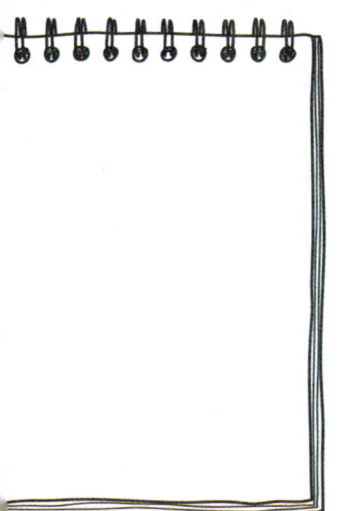   

85. Color the grid as per the given instructions.

If the word is a person, color it green.
If the word is a place, color it red.
If the word is a thing, color it orange.
If the word is an animal or a bird, color it blue.

A **Noun** is a word that denotes the name of a person, place, animal, thing, or an idea.

Sparrow	Deer	Island	Sock
Pen	Shelf	Grandma	Kid
Girl	House	Lake	Saucer
Desk	Caterpillar	Plant	Man
River	Cave	Banana	Policewoman
Dog	Pearl	Panda	Ship

86. Circle the adjectives in each sentence.

Any word that describes the quality of a noun is called an **Adjective**.

1. Shelly is a short girl.

2. I like fluffy puppies.

3. Johnny is a hardworking child.

4. I am wearing a beautiful dress today.

87. Circle verbs with blue color in the given sentences.

They ran all the way home.

 I lit the candles.

He bakes the cake in an oven.

 I am selling books.

I lost my eraser.

Verb

a word or group of words that is used to indicate that something happens o exists, for example bring, happen, be, do.

88. Name the pictures with the correct double letter words.

89. Write the plural forms of the following words.

Frame _____

Bench _____

Thief _____

Brush _____

90. Look at the pictures and circle the right answers.

Kaira is putting on her favorite -
Hairbands, Hairband

The rainbow has seven -
Color, Colors

She combs her -
Hairs, Hair

91. Write the opposites of the following.

Clean _____

Difficult _____

Right _____

Soft _____

Enemy _____

92. Fill in the blanks with the correct prepositions from the box.

on
in
near
between
under

1. The bag is _____ the table.

2. The bird is _____ the sheet.

3. The cat is _____ the bed.

4. The gift is _____ the bed and dog.

5. The table is _____ the room.

93. Match the contractions with the words.

Are not   •   • We'd

we would   •   • They've

there is   •   • Aren't

they have   •   • There's

who is   •   • He'd

he had   •   • Who's

94. Circle the noun.

My sister enjoys watching television.

95. Fill in the blanks using the given words.

| Firewoman | Teacher | Author | Pilot |

She teaches in a school. She is a _____ .

He flies the airplane. He is a _____ .

She puts out the fire. She is a _____ .

He writes books. He is an _____ .

96. Look at the images and complete the sentences.

1. The man is picking _____ from the garden.

2. I like drinking _____ in the morning.

3. The _____ walks very slowly.

97. Fill in the blanks using the 'WH' words.

WH words are a group of English words used to introduce questions. These are what, when, where, which, who, why, and how.

_____ did you go?

_____ was the name of your friend?

_____ gave you this book?

_____ is your birthday?

_____ did you not do your homework?

98. Find the given words in the word search.

E	K	Q	V	N	B	H	Q	P
S	C	L	E	A	N	C	M	L
L	F	S	H	M	N	U	C	A
E	Z	C	E	C	I	Q	P	Y
E	H	E	A	R	T	E	A	X
P	D	F	L	D	P	N	B	G
F	I	T	T	N	I	O	K	W
D	K	T	H	E	W	L	F	P

FIT   HEALTH   PLAY   SLEEP

HEART   CLEAN

99. Complete the dialogue between the hen and the little chick using the given words.

What
Where
Bathe
River

Hen: _____ are you going, little one?

Chick: I am going to the _____.

Hen: _____ will you do there?

Chick: I will _____.

100. With the help of the images, fill in the blanks with the right sound blends (br/bl/cr/cl).

[ ]ock

[ ]ayon

[ ]ain

[ ]ock

[ ]own

[ ]oud

[ ]anket

[ ]ab

[ ]ue

[ ]own

101. Convert the words in the brackets into adverbs and fill in the blanks.

An adverb is a word that modifies a verb, an adjective, or another adverb. Most adverbs are formed by adding -ly in the end.
For example: Slowly, sadly, etc.

1. It is raining (slow) _____.

2. Yesterday, I (accident) _____ swallowed my chewing gum.

3. He was looking at me (anxious) _____.

4. I (usual) _____ go to the gym in the morning.

102. Fill in the blanks with correct pronouns.

Pronouns
Any word that is used in place of a noun is called a pronoun. She, you, him, them, this and us are to name a few.

1. I am looking for Clara. Have you seen _____?

2. Jack has left the class. Where did _____ go?

3. Tara and I are leaving for our dance class. Can you give _____ a ride?

4. I am working. Please don't disturb _____.

103. Fill in the blanks with "is" or "are".

1. How many fruits _____ there in the fridge?

2. Where _____ your homework?

3. This _____ a beautiful car!

4. There _____ five children in the class.

5. Where _____ my books?

104. Complete the following sentences with "must" or "mustn't".

1. You _____ raise your hand to speak.

2. You _____ speak loudly in class.

3. The students _____ complete their homework.

4. You _____ forget your notebook at home.

5. You _____ use your mobile phone in the classroom.

6. You _____ eat your lunch.

105. Circle the correct verb.

 She keep/keeps her room neat and tidy.

 Children usually want/wants to eat cookies.

 My mother play/plays golf on Saturdays.

 They go/goes to church on Wednesdays.

 Henry make/makes delicious food.

 This group of girls like/likes to play football.

106. Where is the orange? Match the images with the correct prepositions.

Behind

In

Under

On

Beside

107. Number the words in each row in alphabetical order.

MOON	LION	REST	KITE	AFTER

ZEBRA	SPIDER	QUEUE	HIDE	FOG

108. Match the collective nouns with the correct picture.

A collection of •   •

A bouquet of •   •

A bowl of •   •

A loaf of •   •

A chest of •   •

A slice of •   •

109. Write few lines about your time in the park.

_____

_____

_____

_____

_____

_____

110. Write the plurals of the following words.

PERSON ....

MOUSE ....

LEAF ....

OX ....

111. Unscramble the sentences and write them correctly.

1. in/always/visit/Manali/We/winters.

_____

2. interesting/Your/more/than/book/ is/mine.

_____

112. Choose the right verb.

1. Pamella (eat, eats) chocolates. _____

2. John (wears, wear) a brown jacket. _____

3. The woman (shouts, shout) out loud. _____

4. The elephant's calves (cry, cries) loudly. _____

5. I (come, comes) here every day. _____

6. The three boys (walk, walks) early in the morning. _____

113. Fill in the blanks correctly with "he", "them", "she", and "they".

1. Clara has many toys. She keeps _____ in a carton.

2. Johnny loves to play football. _____ is playing in the playground.

3. Minnie likes to read. _____ is reading her favorite book.

4. Jack and Jill went up the hill. _____ fell down.

114. Use the correct preposition (in, on, under, above) to fill in the blanks.

The cat is sitting _____ the table.

His grades are _____ average.

The cat likes to sit _____ the box.

Please keep the cups _____ the desk.

115. Color the rhyming words.

PAINT	Rent	Taint	Pint
FUN	Pen	Ten	Run

116. Write 3 words that end with:

ment	red
....	....
....	....
....	....

117. Connect the question words with correct sentences.

Who • • time is it?

Where • • are you?

Which • • is your best friend?

How • • are you crying?

What • • are your glasses?

Why • • one do you want?

118. Write synonyms for the following words.

Beautiful	Small	Afraid
_____	_____	_____

Sad	Happy	Pleasing
_____	_____	_____

119. Write the meanings of the idioms.

1. Tie the knot ....

2. A drop in the bucket ....

3. Cross your fingers ....

4. Get cold feet ....

5. I'm all ears ....

120. Replace the underlined words with their antonyms and rewrite the sentences.

1. The lake is deep. ....

2. They are friends. ....

3. The baby is asleep. ....

121. Fill in the blanks with "have" or "has".

She _____ a new keyboard.

Ella _____ your pencil.

I _____ a question.

We _____ lived in the country for five years.

You _____ a beautiful house.

She _____ been working continuously today.

122. Choose the correct word to complete the sentences.

1. I see Macy every day in my _____ Psychology class.

   i. A   ii. An   iii. The iv. No word

2. Could I please have _____ glass of water?

   i. A   ii. An   iii. The iv. No word

3. It is raining outside. Can you lend me _____ umbrella?

   i. A   ii. An   iii. The iv. No word

4. This is _____ interesting show. You should watch it.

   i. A   ii. An   iii. The iv. No word

123. Circle the preposition and color the picture.

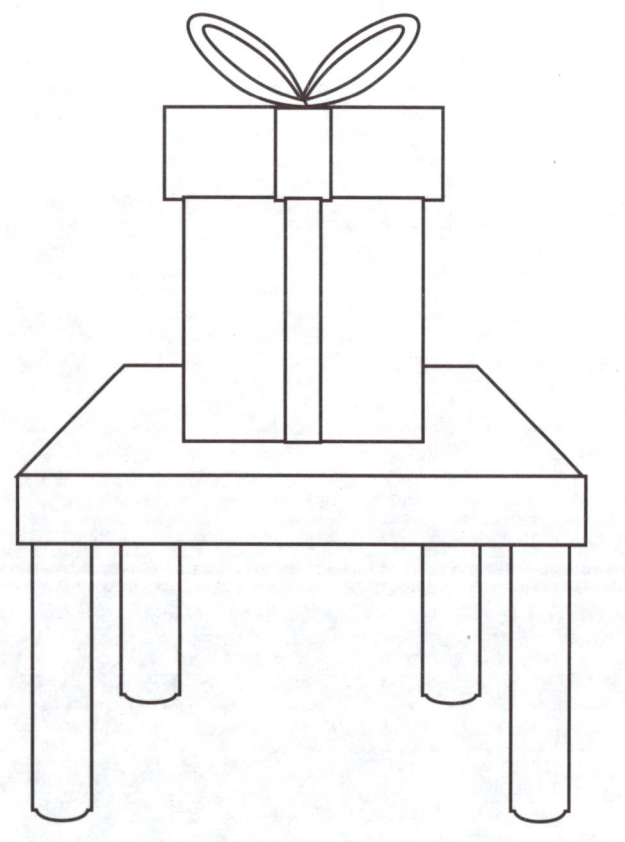

The gift is on the table.

124. What do you like to eat?

I love to eat _____

_____

because _____

_____.

On my birthday, my parents always

get me _____ to eat.

During the winters, I love to eat

_____ because

_____.

I would love to cook _____

_____ one day.

125. Read and answer the following questions.

> Hi. My name is Sara. A week ago, my dad brought me a new pet. It is a cute little puppy. It is two months old. I call it Dodo.
> Dodo loves to sleep as much as he loves to play. My mom and dad help me tend to Dodo and keep him clean. My mom helped me make a kennel for him. Every day after school, I take Dodo for a walk. I love Dodo.

1. When did Sara's dad bring her a new pet?

_____

2. What did Sara name her puppy?

_____

3. What does her new pet love to do?

_____

126. Find the rhyming words from each row.

Rode	Table	Cent	Cable
Game	Name	Blurred	Write
Threw	Giant	Throw	Low
Leak	Late	Speak	Loop
Run	Tons	Lot	Bun
Call	Cell	Shell	Curl

127. Write 3 adjectives to describe yourself.

_____

_____

_____

128. Write 3 adjectives to describe your best friend.

_____

_____

_____

129. Brush up your vocabulary! Choose the correct word meaning.

1. To sniff means to: a. touch   b. feel   c. smell

2. To gather is to: a. buy   b. collect   c. push

3. Swift action means: a. Quiet action   b. Quick action c. Slow action

4. Jovial means: a. Cheerful   b. Sad   c. Melancholy

130. Read aloud the given words. Identify the silent letters and write them in the space.

WRECK   _____

KNEW   _____

REIGN   _____

GNOME   _____

HEIGHT   _____

TAUGHT   _____

HOURGLASS   _____

131. Complete the following sentences by choosing the correct option.

1. My feet am/is/are hairy.

_____

2. I have got/has got some bread.

_____

3. My face am/is/are round.

_____

4. I am/is/are 5 feet tall.

_____

5. My teeth am/is/are white.

_____

132. Fill in the blanks with the correct homophones.

1. I can _____ my dog barking.

(Hear/Here)

2. I _____ the soccer game at

school. (One/Won)

3. Can you _____ your name?

(Write/Right)

133. Use your writing skills and complete the incomplete sentences.

1. I ate a sandwich that

_____

_____.

2. The weather outside was

_____

_____.

3. I hear the dog

_____

_____.

134. Put rhyming words in each basket and write them in their columns.

SNAKE   MOUSE
BRIGHT NARROW
BUNCH   SINK

BASKET 1

PINK   SPARROW
LUNCH   HOUSE
LIGHT   BAKE

BASKET 2

135. Arrange the words in alphabetical order.

Party	1.
Cub	2.
Astronaut	3.
Horse	4.
Ball	5.
Rose	6.
Nose	7.
King	8.
Gun	9.
Ship	10.

136. Solve the crossword for aquatic life.

137. Complete the sentences with the most suitable adverbs.

Outside   Totally   Beautifully
Quickly   Nicely   Well   Quite   Early

1. She always speaks _____.

2. She _____ gets me.

3. The children love to play

_____.

4. He plays the piano

_____.

5. She arrived _____ for the

meeting.

6. He ate the entire meal

_____.

33

138. List 8 things that you see in the given image.

139. Write 5 sentences about your school.

_____

_____

_____

_____

_____

_____

_____

_____

_____

_____

_____

_____

140. Which is your favorite subject and why?

141. Who is your best friend in school. Write 2 lines to describe them.

142. Who is your favorite teacher and why?

143. Observe the images and write what action is taking place in each.

[ ]

[ ]

[ ]

[ ]

144. Tick the word that best describes the sentences given below.

The ones who teaches in school.

Teacher	Joker	Nurse	Doctor
[ ]	[ ]	[ ]	[ ]

The opposite of happy.

Sad	Joy	Angry	Hurt
[ ]	[ ]	[ ]	[ ]

The one who sews your clothes.

Tailor	Gardener	Cobbler	Guard
[ ]	[ ]	[ ]	[ ]

145. Unscramble the jumbled sentences.

1. homework/their/They/always/do.

_____

_____

2. TV/morning/the/We/usually/in/watch/don't.

_____

_____

3. half/The/doctor/past/here/seven/often/at/is.

_____

_____

146. Name five clothes that you wear in winter and summer.

SUMMER

....

....

WINTER

....

....

147. Color the rhyming words.

CHEW	Sew	Free	Queue	Brew

PET	Cat	Rat	Set	Mat

148. Be creative! Use the given words in your own sentences.

RAINBOW _____

JOKER _____

SHOES _____

PUPPY _____

149. Brush up your vocabulary! Choose the correct word meaning.

WEAK   i. Strong   ii. Frail   iii. Sturdy

OLD   i. Fun   ii. Young   iii. Aged

RICH   i. Wealthy   ii. Poor   iii. Dim

BUY   i. Sell   ii. Sold   iii. Purchase

150. Write plurals of the following.

Watch _____

Address _____

Woman _____

151. Find mistakes and rewrite the correct sentences in the blank spaces.

1. These is Penny's favorite toy car.

----

2. My friends and I is good at skateboarding.

----

3. Is this a river in your town?

----

4. A dog is cleverer then a hamster.

----

152. Match the idioms to their meanings.

A dark horse •   • Unable to see well

A copycat •   • Someone who isn't favored in a group

To smell a rat •   • To be pleasant and caring

As blind as a bat •   • A surprise competitor

A black sheep •   • Someone who copies others

As gentle as a lamb •   • To detect something suspicious

153. Replace the underlined words with their antonyms and write the word.

1. It was a cold day.   _____

2. My father braids my curly hair every morning.   _____

3. He got the answer right.   _____

4. Cathy's game is better than Carl's game.   _____

5. Can you please place the warm bowl on the table?   _____

6. The strawberry tasted incredibly sweet.   _____

154. Fill in the blanks with suitable pronouns.

1. Ronit is buying a gift for his friends. _____ is going to give _____ a flower vase.

2. Please don't trouble that dog. _____ may bite _____.

155. Complete the sentences using the correct option.

1. I will _____ you at the game. (meet, meat)

2. What did you _____ from the supermarket? (buy, bye)

156. Match the opposites.

 BIG

 CLEAN

 QUIET

 HAPPY

 SPRING

 DIRTY

 SAD

 AUTUMN

 SMALL

 LOUD

157. Identify and place the gender nouns in the correct columns.

Daughter   Son   Gentleman   Goose
Horse   Mare   Queen   Aunt
Father   Uncle   Niece   Nephew

FEMININE	MASCULINE

158. Choose the correct nouns to complete the following sentences.

1. The _____ is made of wood.

i. Chair   ii. Jacket   iii. Clay

2. I wore a pretty _____.

i. Candle   ii. Door   iii. Dress

3. It's very hot. Could you please switch on the _____?

i. Fan   ii. Leaves   iii. Geyser

4. The king wears a _____ on his head.

i. Throne   ii. Crown   iii. Castle

159. Complete the sentences using the correct option.

Happy   Hot   Mouse   Shut

The tea is _____, but the juice is cold.

The window is _____, but the door is open.

An elephant is big, but a _____ is small.

Honey is _____, but Sheena is sad.

160. Complete the sentences below using a/an.

1. This is _____ bat.

2. This is _____ apple.

3. That is _____ big boat.

4. This is _____ astronaut.

5. This is _____ fish.

6. She has _____ idea.

7. My mother is _____ good cook.

8. My friend has _____ dog.

161. Choose the correct option and complete the sentences.

1. The wind _____ (blue/blew) the leaves.

2. I'll _____ (meet/meat) my friend today.

3. Can we go to the _____ (fair/ fare) today?

4. I have _____ (scene/seen) the movie.

5. Is that a _____ (bee/be) on the flower?

162. Solve the crossword using picture clues.

163. Fill in the blanks with the correct noun.

1. There are uncountable _____ (star/stars) in the sky.

2. Will you be taking the _____? (stairs/stair)

3. Kevin's favorite _____ (book/books) is *The Happy Prince*.

4. John has a brown _____. (dogs/dog)

5. A rainbow has seven _____. (colors/color)

6. The _____ (cats/cat) is sitting on the table.

164. Where are they?

Where is the rabbit?
a. On the table
b. Next to the table
c. Under the table

Where is the dog?
a. Behind the box
b. Next to the box
c. Under the box

Where is the cat?
a. Next to the boxes
b. Behind the boxes
c. Between the boxes

165. Fill in the correct question words in the following sentences.

1. _____ is your hobby?

2. _____ will you return?

3. _____ is playing with the dog?

4. _____ do you do in the evening?

5. _____ cat is in the tree?

6. _____ many fruits are there in the basket?

166. It is the color of the sky.

167. It helps stick things together.

168. You can sit on it.

169. You go here to learn.

170. Use the words in the box to complete the story.

FAVORITE   NAME   BAKE   CAKES
AUNT'S   BAKER

Hi. My _____ is Ahana. I am a

_____. I can _____ all kinds of

cookies, _____, and muffins. My

personal _____ is the chocolate

cake. I work in my _____ bakery.

171. Use your imagination and write a few sentences on the given topic.

Children

_____

_____

_____

_____

_____

_____

172. Read the story and answer the questions.

It is Tyler's birthday today. His mom and dad are planning to give him a surprise birthday party after school. Tyler leaves for school at 9 am. At school, he enjoys a delicious lunch with his friends in the cafeteria. When he returns home, he sees a huge cake on the table. His mom and dad sing "Happy Birthday" for him. Tyler blows out the candles, makes a wish, cuts a piece of the cake, and pops it into his mouth.

1. Who plans Tyler's surprise birthday party?

_____

2. What happens at school?

_____

3. What happens when Tyler comes home?

_____

173. Tick the correct form of verb in the following sentences.

1. Horses don't/doesn't eat meat.

2. When do/does you swim in the pool?

3. Dogs don't climb/doesn't climb trees.

4. Do you drinks/drink milk in the morning?

5. Cathy do/does her homework at noon.

6. Lily goes/go to school every day.

174. Say the following words out loud. Identify the silent letters in them.

Caught   _____

Hour   _____

Honor   _____

Knives   _____

Tomb   _____

175. Fill in the missing comparatives.

A **Comparative** adjective is a word that describes a noun by comparing it to another noun. Comparative adjectives typically end in 'er' and are followed by the word 'than'.

Quick	
Happy	
Fast	
Short	
Thin	
Soft	
Wide	
Fair	

176. Rewrite the sentences by using the contractions for the underlined words.

1. We <u>have not</u> painted the wall.

_____

2. <u>Let us</u> go to the hospital.

_____

3. Reading this book <u>should not</u> take long.

_____

4. <u>We will</u> go home now.

_____

5. Please <u>do not</u> ring the bell.

_____

177. Rewrite the sentences with the correct possessive noun. One has been done for you.

1. The teeth of a shark are sharp.

   A shark's teeth are sharp.

2. The body of a tiger has stripes.

   _____

3. The baby of a giraffe is called a calf.

   _____

A **Possessive noun** is a noun that shows ownership of something. Possessive nouns are generally formed by adding an apostrophe and 's' at the end of a noun.
For example: This is the cat's toy.

178. Match the columns to form complete meaningful sentences.

My baby sister was •   • watch a movie.

Her best friend lives •   • homework, you can't go out to play.

We are going to •   • with a cup of coffee.

If you don't finish your •   • born on 7 April 2006.

I love eating donuts •   • in California.

179. Can you put the right punctuation mark in the following sentences?

1. When is your birthday

_____

2. My favorite subject is English

_____

3. Oh no it's raining

_____

4. It's such a beautiful dress I will buy it

_____

5. May I have a glass of water

_____

180. The given sentences have errors. Rewrite the correct sentences in the space provided.

1. she makes us Cookies for every friday.

- - - - - - - - - - - - - - - - - - - -

2. my dad's name is james brown.

- - - - - - - - - - - - - - - - - - - -

3. Can I borrow your bicycle.

- - - - - - - - - - - - - - - - - - - -

4. What should I get four mom on her birthday

- - - - - - - - - - - - - - - - - - - -

181. Write 2 adverbs to describe "run".

182. Write any 2 adjectives that start with the letter "B".

183. Write 5 nouns that start with the letter "S".

184. Recall and write the pronouns used for the male gender.

185. Replace the underlined words with suitable pronouns and rewrite the sentences.

1. I told my father that I would meet <u>my father</u> at the crossing.

----

2. The pencil was broken when I found <u>the pencil.</u>

----

3. <u>My friends and I</u> want to play in the ground.

----

186. Which part of speech describes the underlined words?

1. I always <u>walk</u> to school.   a. Verb   b. Noun   c. Adjective

2. Grandma baked <u>delicious</u> cookies. a. Verb   b. Noun   c. Adjective

3. <u>Jenny</u> ate an apple.   a. Verb   b. Noun   c. Adjective

4. She's looking for the <u>red</u> book. a. Verb   b. Noun   c. Adjective

5. The baby <u>drank</u> milk.   a. Verb   b. Noun   c. Adjective

187. Sort the vegetables in the correct category.

Cabbage Onion Radish Carrot

Asparagus Spinach Turnip

Ginger Celery Beetroot

Tomato Lettuce

Roots	Stems	Leaves

188. Circle the action words in the following sentences.

1. They bought a new car.

2. Joseph painted the house blue.

3. My dog barked at the burglar.

4. Sam is throwing the ball.

5. I wrote a letter to my friend.

6. Can you teach me how to swim?

189. What group is it?

| Drop | Piece | Tube | Pile | Deck |
| Bunch | Fleet | Chest | | |

A _____ of keys.

A _____ of jewelry.

A _____ of money.

A _____ of rain.

A _____ of drawers.

A _____ of cards.

A _____ of vehicles.

A _____ of toothpaste.

190. Fill in the following blanks with "to", "too", or "two".

Daniel ran ____ miles today.

I love ____ play basketball.

Could you please help me ____?

He got ____ carried away during the performance.

I am going ____ read a book.

We're planning to bring home ____ puppies.

She is ____ far away from home.

191. Complete the tongue-twisters using words from the box. Try saying these tongue-twisters out loud!

| Flea | Socks | Swan |

Swan swam over the sea,
Swim, _____, swim!
Swan swam back again
Well swum, swan!

A flea and a fly flew up
In a flue.
Said the _____, "Let us fly!"
Said the fly, "Let us flee!"
So they flew through a
Flap in the flue.

Susan shines shoes and _____;
Socks and shoes shines Susan.
She ceased shining shoes and socks,
For shoes and socks shock Susan.

192. I have two wheels and a bell in front,
Ride me to stay fit or perform stunt.
What am I?

193. Rectangular in shape with six wheels,
I carry students to school in all zeals.
What am I?

194. I am not a bird in the sky,
But I have wings and I fly.
What am I?

195. Petrol or diesel on long ride,
Four wheels on road, "roll tide"!
What am I?

196. Practice your writing skills.

1. I am good at _____
_____.

2. I am bad at _____
_____.

3. I don't like _____
because _____.

4. I like _____
because _____.

5. I love to play _____
_____.

6. I don't like to play _____
_____.

7. My favorite movie is _____
because _____.

197. Find the names of wildlife you spot at zoo.

L	H	X	C	V	N	X	T	H	P
I	S	G	I	R	A	F	F	E	A
O	W	A	N	L	X	N	M	O	R
N	I	B	W	U	D	I	N	O	R
X	R	A	U	X	G	I	U	Y	O
Z	K	E	T	H	A	O	B	T	
T	I	G	E	R	O	L	T	U	Z
M	A	O	K	N	Q	S	G	M	A
E	O	O	W	M	O	N	K	E	Y
O	G	G	E	V	Y	C	V	Q	A

Monkey Giraffe Tiger Rhino
Lion Emu Parrot

198. Pick the nouns from the box and place them in the correct category.

Teacher Toothpaste Carpet Ladybug
Mother Catfish Hospital School Police
Nurse Theater Station Barber Cow
Dog Pen Book

PERSON	PLACE	THING	ANIMAL

199. Fill in appropriate words to complete the sentences.

Oceans Marine Water
Cold-blooded Rivers Reptiles

Fishes are _____ animals. They can be found in

_____ or _____. Fish need _____ to

live. These animals are just like _____. They are also

_____.

200. Color the clouds that are feminine.

Madam   King   Lioness   Tiger

Siri   Doe   Policewoman   Prince

201. Fill in the blanks with suitable words from the box.

Arms Happy Sing Toes
Room Bed Dinner

Suzy is a _____ child. She loves to dance and _____. Every day

after school, she practices dance in her _____. She lifts her _____

and points her _____ just like a ballerina. She practices until her

father calls her for _____. After dinner, little Suzy goes to _____.

202. Read the following passage and rearrange the jumbled sentences given below.

Once upon a time there was a mother dog and her little puppy. They lived happily on a farm. The puppy was black with white spots and very playful. One day, he walked on the road and almost got hit by a car. "Don't walk in the road again until you grow up and learn how to cross a street," said Mamma Dog. "A long time ago, when I was just a little puppy, I got hit by a car. Luckily, it didn't hurt me too bad. I learned how to cross the road safely then on. I look both ways and I cross only if I don't see or hear a car coming," added Mamma Dog. "Yes, Mom, I learned a good lesson today," answered the little puppy.

1. a / got / by / car / I / hit

_____

2. The / spots / with / puppy / was / white / black

_____

3. Don"t / the / in / walk / road

_____

4. lesson / today / I / a / good / learned

_____